TECUMSEH

Have You Seen My Mother?

Illustrations by Yutaka Sugita
Story by Anne Maley

CAROLRHODA BOOKS INC.
MINNEAPOLIS, MINNESOTA U.S.A.

First published in the United States 1969 by CAROLRHODA BOOKS, INC.,
Minneapolis, Minnesota. All United States and Canadian rights reserved.

Illustrations only Copyright © 1966 by SHIKO-SHA, Tokyo, Japan.

International Standard Book Number: 0-87614-001-0
Library of Congress Catalog Card Number: 76-82448

Printed in Japan and bound in the United States.

Second Printing 1971

Have You Seen My Mother?

One summer afternoon, a bright ball named Barnabus
lay in a circus tent and dreamed.
He dreamed that he had a mother.
The dream was so real that it woke Barnabus up.
He wondered,
"Do I have a mother?"
Perhaps the circus animals would know.

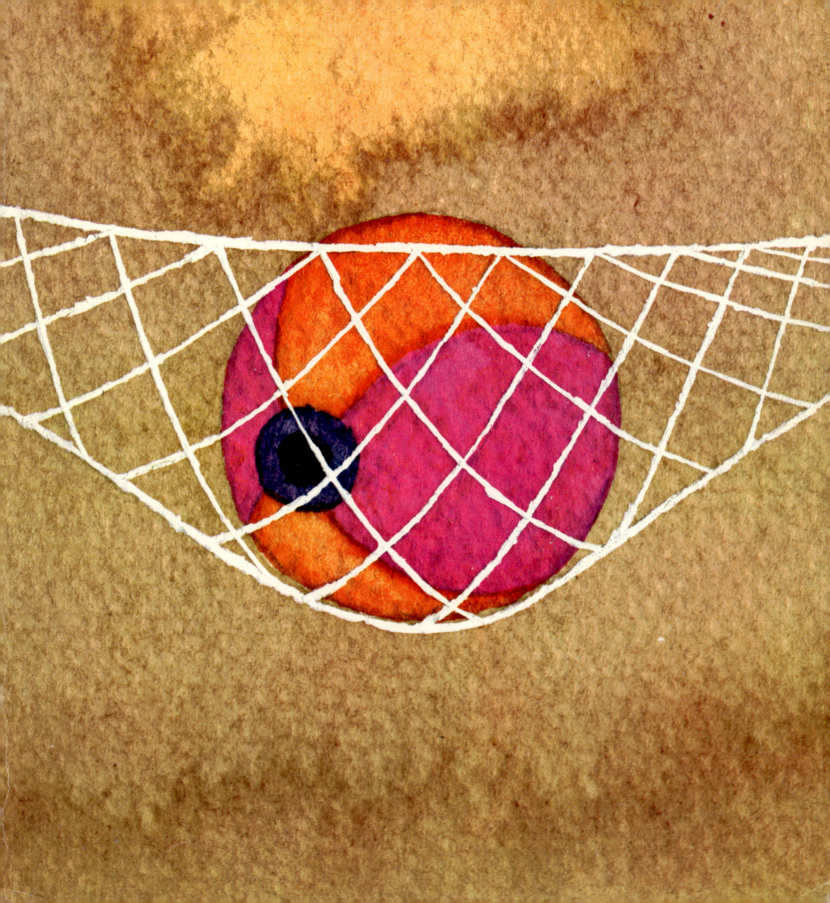

He asked the camel first,
"Have you seen my mother?"

The camel blinked. "I was not aware that balls had mothers. Camels do, of course," he said.

Barnabus asked a small dachshund,
"Have *you* seen my mother?"

"No," said the dachshund. "But *my* mother is here. Would you like to meet her?"

"How do you do," said Barnabus politely, and bounced on.

Barnabus asked a parrot,
"Have *you* seen my mother?"

But the parrot mother did not answer.
She wanted to talk about her children.
"I cover them with my wings to keep them together," she said.

"Have *you* seen my mother?" Barnabus
asked a seal. "Is she hiding in the water?"

"Only the fish and I are in the water,"
said the seal.

Barnabus asked a kangaroo,
"Have *you* seen my mother?
Is she hiding in your pouch?"

"You may look — if you are careful,"
said the mother kangaroo.

So Barnabus looked inside the warm dark pouch
and saw a baby kangaroo sleeping there.

"O wise King Lion, *you* must have seen my mother," said Barnabus.

"No!" roared the lion,
and the force of his voice blew Barnabus away.

"Have *you* seen my mother?" Barnabus
asked the zebra.

"Balls don't need mothers,
but I need a playmate," said the zebra.
"Stop and play with me."

But Barnabus went on.

Finally Barnabus had asked all of the animals except the tigers.
"Have *you* seen my mother?" asked Barnabus.

"She is not in this circus," the tigers growled.
"You will have to look elsewhere."

Barnabus was sad. "If I could go out into the world,
I might find my mother there," he said.

A clown heard Barnabus and bounced
him high into the air.

Barnabus soared above the circus tents,
straight up through the sky,
high enough to reach the sun.

He looked at the sun and saw that it was
a bright ball like himself.

"Oh Sun, YOU are my mother!" cried Barnabus.
The sun laughed and said, "YES."

On summer afternoons, a bright ball named
Barnabus lies in a circus tent and dreams.
He dreams of his mother — the warm, bright sun.
And when he awakes, she is always there.

About the author...

Anne Maley is a graduate of Clarke College in Dubuque, Iowa, with a major in music. She has been both a music teacher and consultant in the Michigan elementary schools. For the past five years she has been an editor and writer of educational materials. Miss Maley is particularly interested in writing stories and composing music for young children.

About the artist...

The illustrations in this book are by the distinguished Japanese artist Yutaka Sugita. Mr. Sugita is rapidly gaining international stature for his illustrations which feature color used in a bold and imaginative way. Mr. Sugita is known as the Japanese Brian Wildsmith.

CAROLRHODA BOOKS

241 FIRST AVENUE NORTH — MINNEAPOLIS, MINNESOTA 55401

Published in memory of Carolrhoda Locketz Rozell,
Who loved to bring children and books together

Please write for a complete catalogue